ish

Peter H. Reynolds

WALKER BOOKS
AND SUBSIDIARIES

LONDON • BOSTON • SYDNEY • AUCKLAND

Ramon loved to draw.

Any time.

Anything.

Anywhere.

One day, Ramon was drawing
a vase of flowers.
His brother, Leon,
leaned over his shoulder.

Leon burst out laughing.
"WHAT is THAT?" he asked.

Ramon could not even answer.
He just crumpled up the drawing
and threw it across the room.

Leon's laughter haunted Ramon.
He kept trying to make his
drawings look "right",
but they never did.

After many months and
many crumpled sheets of paper,
Ramon put his pencil down.

"I'm done."

Marisol, his sister, was watching him.
"What do YOU want?" he snapped.

"I was watching you draw," she said.

Ramon sneered.
"I'm NOT drawing! Go away!"

Marisol ran away, but not before
picking up a crumpled sheet of paper.

"Hey! Come back here with that!"

Ramon raced after Marisol,
up the hall and into her room.

He was about to yell
but fell silent when
he saw his sister's walls...
He stared at the crumpled gallery.

"This is one of my favourites,"
Marisol said, pointing.

"That was SUPPOSED to be a
vase of flowers," Ramon said,
"but it doesn't look like one."

"Well, it looks vase-ISH!"
she exclaimed.

"Vase-ISH?"

Ramon looked closer.
Then he studied all the drawings on
Marisol's walls and began to
see them in a whole new way.

"They do look...ish," he said.

Ramon felt light and energized.
Thinking ish-ly allowed
his ideas to flow freely.

He began to draw what he felt—
loose lines.
Quickly springing out.
Without worry.

Ramon once again drew
and drew the world around him.
Making an ish drawing
felt wonderful.

He filled his notebooks...

tree-ish

house-ish

boat-ish

afternoon-ish

fish-ish

sun-ish

Ramon realized he could draw ish feelings too.

peace-ish

silly-ish

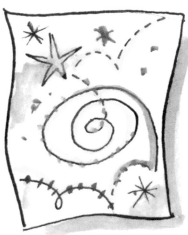

excited-ish.

His ish art inspired ish writing.
He wasn't sure if he was writing poems,
but he knew they were poem-ish.

One spring morning,
Ramon had a wonderful feeling.
It was a feeling that even ish words
and ish drawings could not capture.
He decided NOT to capture it.
Instead, he simply savoured it...

And Ramon lived ishfully ever after.

The End-ish

Dedicated to Doug Kornfeld, my art teacher, who
dared me to draw for myself and find my voice

First published 2004 by Walker Books Ltd
87 Vauxhall Walk, London SE11 5HJ

This edition published 2005

18 20 19 17

© 2004 Peter H. Reynolds

The right of Peter H. Reynolds to be identified as author/illustrator of this work has been
asserted by him in accordance with the Copyright, Designs and Patents Act 1988

This book was handlettered by Peter H. Reynolds

Printed in China

All rights reserved. No part of this book may be reproduced, transmitted or stored in an
information retrieval system in any form or by any means, graphic, electronic or mechanical,
including photocopying, taping and recording, without prior written permission from the publisher.

British Library Cataloguing in Publication Data:
a catalogue record for this book is available from the British Library

ISBN 978-1-84428-296-8

www.walker.co.uk